A Quiet Night In

TO THE BEST NANNA IN THE WORLD

WITH LOVE FROM US

First published 1993 by Walker Books Ltd
87 Vauxhall Walk, London SE11 5HJ

© 1993 Jill Murphy

This edition published 1998

6 8 10 9 7 5

Printed in Hong Kong

British Library Cataloguing in Publication Data
A catalogue record for this book is available
from the British Library.

ISBN 0-7445-6000-4

A Quiet Night In

Jill Murphy

WALKER BOOKS

AND SUBSIDIARIES

LONDON • BOSTON • SYDNEY

"I want you all in bed early tonight,"
said Mrs Large. "It's Daddy's birthday
and we're going to have a quiet night in."
"Can we be there too?" asked Laura.
"No," said Mrs Large. "It wouldn't be
quiet with you lot all charging about
like a herd of elephants."
"But we *are* a herd of elephants," said Lester.
"Smartypants," said Mrs Large. "Come on
now, coats on. It's time for school."

That evening, Mrs Large had
the children bathed and in their
pyjamas before they had even had
their tea. They were all very cross.
"It's only half past four," said Lester.
"It's not even dark yet."
"It soon will be," said Mrs Large grimly.

After tea, the children set about making
place cards and decorations for the
dinner table. Then they all tidied up.
Then Mrs Large tidied up again.

Mr Large arrived home looking very tired.

"We're all going to bed," said Lester.

"So you can be quiet," said Laura.

"Without us," said Luke.

"Shhhh," said the baby.

"Happy Birthday," said Mrs Large. "Come and see the table."

Mr Large sank heavily into the sofa. "It's lovely, dear," he said, "but do you think we could have our dinner on trays in front of the TV? I'm feeling a bit tired."

"Of course," said Mrs Large. "It's *your* birthday.
   You can have whatever you want."
"We'll help," said Luke.
   The children ran to the kitchen and brought two trays.
"I'll set them," said Mrs Large. "We don't want
   everything ending up on the floor."

"Can we have a story before we
  go to bed?" asked Luke.

"Please," said Lester.

"Go on, Dad," said Laura. "Just one."

"Story!" said the baby.

"Oh, all right," said Mr Large.

"Just one, then."

  Lester chose a book and they all
  cuddled up on the sofa.

Mr Large opened the book and began to read:
"One day Binky Bus drove out of the big garage.
'Hello!' he called to his friend, Micky Milkfloat –"
"I don't like that one," said Laura. "It's a boy's story."
"Look," said Mr Large, "if you're going to argue about it,
you can all go straight to bed without *any* story."
So they sat and listened while Mr Large read to them.

After a while he stopped.

"Go on, Daddy," said Luke.

"What happened after he
bumped into Danny Dustcart?"

"Did they have a fight?" asked Lester.

"Look," said Laura. "Daddy's asleep."

"Shhhh!" said the baby.

Mrs Large laughed. "Poor Daddy," she said.
"Never mind, we'll let him snooze a bit longer
while I take you all up to bed."
"Will you just finish the story, Mum?" asked Lester.
"We don't know what happens in the end," said Luke.
"Please," said Laura.
"Story!" said the baby.

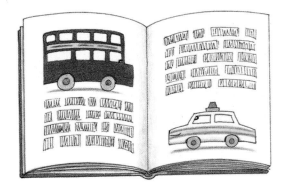

"Move up, then," said Mrs Large. She picked up
the book and began to read: "'Watch where
you're going, you silly Dustcart!' said Binky.
Just then, Pip the Police Car came driving by..."

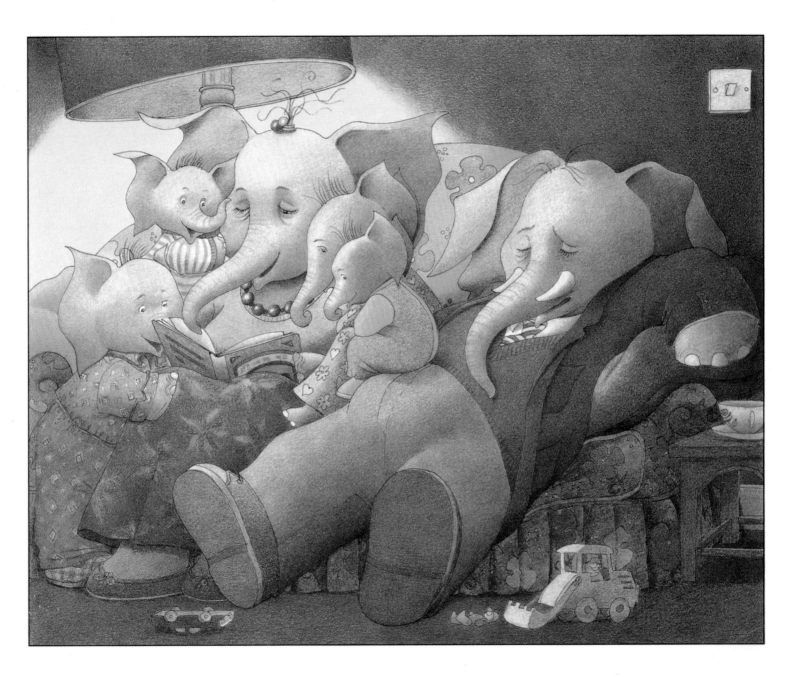

After a while, Mrs Large stopped reading.

"What's that strange noise?" asked Lester.

"It's Mummy snoring," said Luke. "Daddy's snoring too."

"They must be very tired," said Laura, kindly.

"Shhhh!" said the baby.

The children crept from the sofa and fetched a blanket.

They covered Mr and Mrs Large and tucked them in.

"We'd better put ourselves to bed,"
  said Lester. "Come on."
"Shall we take the food up with us?"
  asked Luke. "It *is* on trays."
"It's a pity to waste it," said Laura.
"I'm sure they wouldn't mind. Anyway,
  they wanted a quiet night in."
"Shhhh!" said the baby.

MORE WALKER PAPERBACKS
For You to Enjoy

Some more Large Family books by Jill Murphy

FIVE MINUTES' PEACE

Winner of the Best Book for Babies Award

All Mrs Large wants is a few minutes' peace in the bath away
from the children.
But the little Larges have other ideas!
ISBN 0-7445-6001-2   £4.99

ALL IN ONE PIECE

Highly Commended for the Kate Greenaway Medal

While Mr and Mrs Large get ready to go out for the evening, Laura,
Lester, Luke and the baby are busy making a mess!
ISBN 0-7445-6002-0   £4.99

A PIECE OF CAKE

Mrs Large puts the family on a diet of healthy food and exercise.
But when a cake arrives from Grandma, the family's resolve is sorely tested!
"The illustrations are pure delight… More rueful smiles from mothers everywhere." *The Lady*
ISBN 0-7445-6003-9   £4.99

Walker Paperbacks are available from most booksellers, or by post from B.B.C.S., P.O. Box 941, Hull, North Humberside HU1 3YQ
24 hour telephone credit card line 01482 224626

To order, send: Title, author, ISBN number and price for each book ordered, your full name and address,
cheque or postal order payable to BBCS for the total amount and allow the following for postage and packing:
UK and BFPO: £1.00 for the first book, and 50p for each additional book to a maximum of £3.50.
Overseas and Eire: £2.00 for the first book, £1.00 for the second and 50p for each additional book.
Prices and availability are subject to change without notice.